CHAT

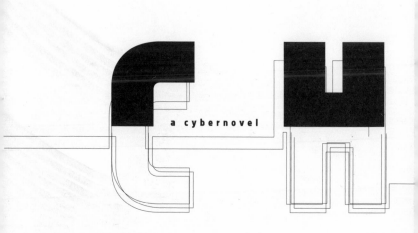

a cybernovel

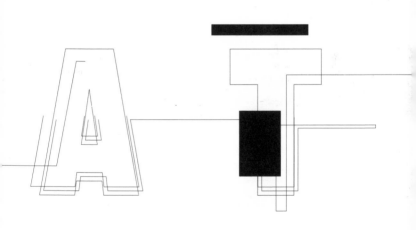

NAN McCARTHY

RAINWATER PRESS   PEACHPIT PRESS

Chat
Nan McCarthy

Copyright © 1996 by Nancy J. McCarthy
All rights reserved.

Peachpit Press
2414 Sixth Street
Berkeley, CA 94710
(510) 548-4393 phone
(510) 548-5991 fax
http://www.peachpit.com

Peachpit Press is a division of Addison Wesley Longman

Cover + Interior Design: David High
Creative Director: Nancy McCarthy
Consulting Editor: Linnea Dayton
Production: Rainwater Press

CHAT is a work of fiction. The characters in it have been invented by the author,
and any resemblance to actual persons, living or dead, is purely coincidental.

ISBN 0-201-88668-5

9 8 7 6 5 4 3 2

Printed in the United States of America.

FOR PAT

"You must do the thing you think you cannot do."
— *Eleanor Roosevelt*

acknowledgments

I would first like to thank the people who actually experienced online romances and who let me interview them for this book. Though they wish to remain anonymous, the insights and intimate details they shared with me helped to make this a much better book than it would have been had they not been so forthcoming.

I would next like to thank the hundreds—if not thousands—of people with whom I have corresponded electronically over the past ten years and who welcomed me into their online communities.

Like many writers, I frequently rely on the encouragement and constructive criticism of friends, family members, and colleagues. I would like to thank the people who were especially helpful to me as I struggled to turn this book into a reality: Joel Sironen, Linnea Dayton, Mike Walsh, David Ambler, David High, Steve Collins, Scott Culley, Barbara Rainwater Redinger, my mom, my sister, and my husband Patrick, who helped me with everything from business decisions to plot and character development. My two sons, Ben and Cole, aren't old enough to offer encouragement in the way that most adults would, but their love and need for me is perhaps the best encouragement of all.

— *Nan McCarthy*

When I first wrote and self-published CHAT in 1995, I felt fairly confident that my computer industry friends and colleagues would get a kick out of it. And although I made a conscious effort to make the book easy to understand and fun for readers who may have never set foot in cyberspace, I still wasn't sure if CHAT would be as big a hit with the rest of the world as it was with the techno-weenies I tend to hang out with. Luckily, I realized my doubts were unfounded as CHAT began selling to a wider audience than I would have ever dared dream.

If you haven't had the experience of logging on to the Internet or to a commercial online service, or even if you don't yet own a computer, you can still ease yourself into the new terminology of this exciting phenomenon by glancing through the brief glossary of abbreviations, acronyms, and emoticons at the back of this book. These shorthand words and symbols help people who are communicating via electronic messages to interject emotion, tone, and even action into a medium that would otherwise be devoid of the valuable signals we often pick up when listening to a person's voice on the telephone or observing facial expressions and body language.

So feel free to familiarize yourself with these easy-to-understand terms by looking at the glossary before you start reading CHAT. Or, you can just dive right in, and refer to the glossary after you've joined Bev and Max on their wild ride through cyberspace.

— *Nan McCarthy*

member profile

Member Name: Beverly J.
ID: BevJ@frederic_gerard.com
Location: Midwest
Birth date: October 11
Sex: Female
Marital Status: Married
Computers: Mac Quadra and a PowerBook
Interests: Reading, playing the piano, studying
         typography
Occupation: Editor
Quote: *Great works are performed not by strength but*
       by perseverance.
                              —*Samuel Johnson*

member profile

Member Name: Maximilian M.
ID: Maximilian@miller&morris.com
Location: Northern Hemisphere
Birth date: Taurus
Sex: male
Marital Status: single
Computers: who cares
Interests: bonsai gardening, writing poetry, mixing
         the perfect martini
Occupation: copywriter
Quote: *For myself I live, live intensely and am fed by*
       life, and my value, whatever it be, is in my
       own kind of expression of that.
                              —*Henry James*

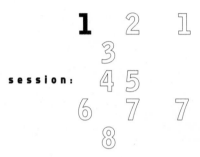

session:

> Private Mail
> Date: Friday, July 14, 1995 1:48 a.m.
> From: Maximilian@miller&morris.com
> Subj: Hello
> To: BevJ@frederic_gerard.com

Beverly, (is that your real name?)

I've seen your messages in the Writer's Forum and you seem to know a lot about computers. I'm thinking of upgrading my old '386 PC and I'm wondering if you can give me any advice on whether I should buy a PC or a Macintosh.

Also, I noticed in your member profile that you're an

editor. Where do you work? I'm a copywriter...maybe we could get together sometime.

Maximilian (that's my real name)

> Private Mail
> Date: Monday, July 17, 1995 7:32 a.m.
> From: BevJ@frederic_gerard.com
> Subj: Thanks, but No Thanks
> To: Maximilian@miller&morris.com

Maximilian:

I really don't like to give advice on whether a person should buy a Mac or a PC, especially because I know nothing about the way you work and what you want to accomplish with your computer. If you're just going to be doing word processing, it probably doesn't matter whether you use a Mac or a PC.

I'm sorry I don't have time to chat but I'm under a lot of deadlines at the moment.

p.s. Just in case you didn't notice, my member profile says I'm married.

> Private Mail
> Date: Monday, July 17, 1995 11:08 a.m.
> From: Maximilian@miller&morris.com
> Subj: Ouch!
> To: BevJ@frederic_gerard.com

Sheesh! You didn't seem so uptight in your messages
on the Writer's Forum! Besides, I wasn't trying to
pick you up—I don't do cybersex, and you could be a
real toad for all I know.

I promise to quit bugging you if you'll just tell me if
Beverly is your real name.

Maximilian

> Private Mail
> Date: Tuesday, July 18, 1995 6:50 a.m.
> From: BevJ@frederic_gerard.com
> Subj: Ouch!
> To: Maximilian@miller&morris.com

Maximilian:

Excuse me? I am not a toad, for your information.
You, on the other hand, are probably wearing a
smelly jogging suit with your butt hanging out the
back and Cheetos crumbs hanging off your beard.

But since you've promised to stop bothering me, I

will tell you that Beverly is my real name. And I am
not uptight, BTW.

Beverly

> Private Mail
> Date: Tuesday, July 18, 1995 10:37 a.m.
> From: Maximilian@miller&morris.com
> Subj: Sorry
> To: BevJ@frederic_gerard.com

Beverly,

Look, I'm really sorry. I had a hangover when I
wrote that message at work yesterday morning. Can
we start over? I swear I wasn't trying to pick you
up... I've just been a copywriter for so long that I
was curious how you got to be an editor.

Maximilian

p.s. I don't wear jogging suits, I don't have a beard,
and I don't even like Cheetos. What does "BTW"
mean? And why did you put asterisks around one of
your words?

> Private Mail
> Date: Wednesday, July 19, 1995 7:23 a.m.
> From: BevJ@frederic_gerard.com
> Subj: Sorry
> To: Maximilian@miller&morris.com

Maximilian:

I thought you said you wanted computer advice, not
career advice? And who's your boss anyway? From the
time on your messages, it looks as if you're strolling
into work just in time to take your lunch break. If
you worked for me, I'd fire your ass in a heartbeat.

Beverly

p.s. You must be new online—"BTW" stands for "by
the way." People use all sorts of acronyms like that
to make typing online faster and easier. The asterisks
are used for emphasis, since you can't type in italics
online. Some people use underscores at the beginning
and end of a word or phrase (_like this_) to mean
the same thing.

> Private Mail
> Date: Thursday, July 20, 1995 11:41 a.m.
> From: Maximilian@miller&morris.com
> Subj: Sorry
> To: BevJ@frederic_gerard.com

OK, so now that we've established we could never

work together, I guess there's not much else to talk about since you seem fairly incapable of having any kind of conversation that's even remotely personal.

(And yes, I'm new to this whole online thing.)

Maximilian

> Private Mail
> Date: Friday, July 21, 1995 8:02 a.m.
> From: BevJ@frederic_gerard.com
> Subj: Truce?
> To: Maximilian@miller&morris.com

Maximilian,

I am not incapable of participating in friendly discussion. It's just that I get a lot of weird e-mail from people I don't even know. Usually people want something from me, like they want me to read their nephew's first novel and help them get it published, or they want computer advice, or sometimes these people are just plain lunatics, and I have to change my e-mail address in order to get away from them. One woman found out where I lived and started calling me at all hours of the night, threatening to commit suicide if I didn't talk to her. The sysops had to lock her out of one of the forums because she was filling up the message boards with all these crazy ramblings, and a bunch of us had to get unlisted phone numbers.

Even the people who just want computer or editorial advice expect me to give away my time for free; they don't understand that I, too, have to work for a living.

Oh well, sorry for the little flame there; I guess you've hit one of my sore spots. <g>

Just so you know—a "flame" is a message from someone who's pissed off and venting a lot of steam; my message is pretty mild compared to some of the flames you see online. A "sysop" is someone who manages a forum (it's short for "system operator"), and the <g> stands for an electronic grin. Because you can't see the expression on people's faces or hear the inflection of their voices when "talking" online, a lot of people use the <g> or :-) (sideways smiley face, called an "emoticon") to show they are joking or trying to be friendly when typing something that could be misconstrued.

Tell you what: Just to show you that I am not a horrible person, I'll let you ask me one question, which I will answer to the best of my knowledge. One question, one answer. Deal?

Beverly

> Private Mail
> Date: Saturday, July 22, 1995 2:14 a.m.
> From: Maximilian@miller&morris.com
> Subj: One Question
> To: BevJ@frederic_gerard.com

Beverly,

It's a deal, and thanks for the background info on
what all that jargon means. I've been wondering what
it all stands for since I got online a few weeks ago,
but have always felt too stupid to ask about it on the
public message boards.

And now... Here's my question:

Are you happy?

2 1 **2**
3
5 4 5
7 7 8

> Private Mail
> Date: Monday, July 24, 1995 5:21 a.m.
> From: BevJ@frederic_gerard.com
> Subj: One Question
> To: Maximilian@miller&morris.com

Maximilian:

Can't we go back to talking about what kind of computer I think you should buy? <g>

Am I happy??? What sort of question is that? Are you sure you're not trying to come on to me?

If you're so intent on getting personal, why don't you

just ask me where I grew up? What my major was in college? What my favorite color is? What kind of food I like, books I read, or even who gave me my first kiss?

Beverly

> Private Mail
> Date: Monday, July 24, 1995 8:57 p.m.
> From: Maximilian@miller&morris.com
> Subj: One Question
> To: BevJ@frederic_gerard.com

Beverly,

Come on! A DEAL IS A DEAL!!!!!

Maximilian

> Private Mail
> Date: Tuesday, July 25, 1995 6:53 a.m.
> From: BevJ@frederic_gerard.com
> Subj: One Question
> To: Maximilian@miller&morris.com

Maximilian:

You're right, a deal is a deal. I'll answer your question on one condition—you quit using your caps lock key when you're typing messages online—people consider it rude because it looks as if you're shouting.

Beverly

> Private Mail
> Date: Tuesday, July 25, 1995 10:31 a.m.
> From: Maximilian@miller&morris.com
> Subj: One Question
> To: BevJ@frederic_gerard.com

OK, Beverly. I'm waaaaitinnnnnng...<g>

> Private Mail
> Date: Wednesday, July 26, 1995 7:12 a.m.
> From: BevJ@frederic_gerard.com
> Subj: One Answer
> To: Maximilian@miller&morris.com

Why do I get the feeling you're enjoying this? I really have gotten myself into some predicament, haven't I? <mutter, mutter>

All right. I'll answer your silly question. Of course I'm happy—mostly. No one is 100% happy, right?

Are *you* happy?

Beverly

> Private Mail
> Date: Wednesday, July 26, 1995 9:22 a.m.
> From: Maximilian@miller&morris.com
> Subj: One More Question
> To: BevJ@frederic_gerard.com

Beverly, (have I told you that's a pretty name?)

I would like to know what would make you 100% happy.

Max

> Private Mail
> Date: Friday, July 28, 1995 11:52 a.m.
> From: Maximilian@miller&morris.com
> Subj: Hello?
> To: BevJ@frederic_gerard.com

Beverly,

So where are you? It's been a couple of days and I haven't heard from you. Did I breach another cyber rule or something with my last message?

Max

> Private Mail
> Date: Friday, July 28, 1995 5:48 p.m.
> From: BevJ@frederic_gerard.com
> Subj: Hello?
> To: Maximilian@miller&morris.com

Maximilian:

No, you didn't breach any more cyber rules. I've had a lot going on at work lately, trying to settle endless disputes between my writers and graphic designers. The writers are upset because the designers keep typesetting their stories in 6-point type, and the designers are upset because the writers won't cut the copy to fit their layouts. I've finally gotten them to compromise: The designers have agreed to set the type in 8 points—still too small IMHO (that's "in my humble opinion" btw)—and the writers have agreed to cut ten lines of their precious copy.

Anyhow, getting back to our topic du jour, there's no way I'm going to answer a second question from you! A deal is a deal, remember? And besides, you never even answered my question, about whether or not *you're* happy.

Beverly

> Private Mail
> Date: Saturday, July 29, 1995 2:02 a.m.
> From: Maximilian@miller&morris.com
> Subj: Hello?
> To: BevJ@frederic_gerard.com

Beverly,

I'm glad to know that I haven't pissed you off again.
I really like talking to you. You probably think I'm
some geek who gets off on trying to pick up chicks
online, but you're the only person I've "met" so far
who seems to have half a brain.

Since I'm the one who started this whole damn
thing, I guess I owe it to you to answer my own
question. To tell you the truth, I'm not very happy at
all, though it would surprise most of the people who
know me to hear me say that. Most people think I'm
a happy-go-lucky guy who happens to be a kick-ass
advertising copywriter making a pretty damn good
living at it.

I've been having a lot of problems at work lately and
I guess that's the reason I'm not happy. The owner of
my ad agency is this total maniac who goes around
making people's lives miserable. Most of us joke
about him behind his back, but when you get right
down to brass tacks, I'm beginning to think he's eating me alive. This is a cut-throat business to begin
with, so I never thought of myself as thin-skinned,
but I'm wondering how much longer I can take it.

What bothers me the most is that my happiness seems to be so closely tied with who I am professionally. Why do so many of us value ourselves based on what we do for a living—on whether our bosses give us a big raise or not and how much our coworkers say they like us?

Ah, well. I didn't mean to get so philosophical on you. I guess it's because it's two in the morning; I just got back from a night on the town with some friends and I think I've had one martini too many.

Maximilian

> Private Mail
> Date: Monday, July 31, 1995 9:02 a.m.
> From: BevJ@frederic_gerard.com
> Subj: Job Stuff
> To: Maximilian@miller&morris.com

No, I don't think you're a geek, Maximilian. In fact I'm actually enjoying talking to you, too. It's a nice break from some of the drivel I have to deal with all day long.

I'm sorry to hear about what you're going through at work. I can honestly say I can relate, because I had a boss like that once. No corporate environment is ever perfect, but the last place I worked added a whole new dimension to the term "dysfunctional."

All I can tell you is that you've got to just continue doing what you think is right. No matter what happens, you want to be able to look at yourself in the mirror in the morning and like what you see.

Take care,
Beverly

> Private Mail
> Date: Monday, July 31, 1995 10:29 a.m.
> From: Maximilian@miller&morris.com
> Subj: Job Stuff
> To: BevJ@frederic_gerard.com

Beverly,

Thanks for the encouragement. So what happened at the last place you worked? Did you quit?

Maximilian

p.s. If you won't tell me what would make you 100% happy, maybe you could just tell me about your first kiss. ;-)

> Private Mail
> Date: Tuesday, August 1, 1995 6:14 a.m.
> From: BevJ@frederic_gerard.com
> Subj: Job Stuff
> To: Maximilian@miller&morris.com

Maximilian:

Check you out—using online emoticons! That sideways wink was pretty impressive. ;-)

Anyhow, to answer your question about the last place
I worked, no, I didn't quit—I was fired. It was really
kind of funny, because, like yours, my self esteem
was largely based on what I accomplished professionally. I worked my ass off, and I was in this constant
state of panic over my job and trying to please my
boss. When I finally got fired, it was actually a huge
relief. The reality of getting fired was much less horrible than the fear of getting fired. My mom used to
quote Franklin Roosevelt when I was a kid—"The
only thing we have to fear is fear itself"—and boy,
was she right.

Beverly

p.s. I can't tell you about my first kiss—I'd be too
embarrassed, and besides, we hardly know each
other!

> Private Mail
> Date: Tuesday, August 1, 1995 10:58 a.m.
> From: Maximilian@miller&morris.com
> Subj: First Kiss
> To: BevJ@frederic_gerard.com

CHICKEN!!! <g>

session:

1
2 **3**
4
6 7 8
9 1

> Tuesday, August 1, 1995 7:13 p.m.

> Writer's Forum > Live Conference > People Here: 9

DonA(Mod): For those of you who just joined us, the
topic of tonight's live CO is how to
find a job as an advertising copywriter.
First I'd like to briefly go over a few of
the rules of live conference etiquette...
If you would like to ask a question or
make a comment, type a ? (question
mark) or a ! (exclamation point). As the
moderator, I will tell you to go ahead
with a "GA" followed by your name. If

	you all behave yourselves, I won't interject too much.
ThomH:	?
DonA(Mod):	GA, Thom.
ThomH:	Is there anyone here who already works in advertising?
BevJ:	!
DonA(Mod):	GA, Bev.
BevJ:	Maximilian is a copywriter—or so he claims. <g,d&rvvf>
ThomH:	?
Maximilian:	!
DonA(Mod):	GA, Thom, then GA Maximilian.
ThomH:	Maximilian, are you really a copywriter?
Maximilian:	My boss might disagree, but yes, I'm a professional copywriter. (Thanks for your support, Bev.) <g>
ThomH:	I'll be graduating from college next spring, but I have no idea how to start looking for a job. Any thoughts?
Maximilian:	Aside from the things that your college placement office should be doing for you, such as job-search seminars and the like, you could start looking for a position as an intern. Agencies love to hire interns, because it's cheap labor, yet you're all a bunch of eager beavers. <g> You won't get rich, but you're sure to get some useful experience and make some even more useful contacts.
ThomH:	Hmm. I hadn't thought of doing an internship. How did you get started in the biz?

Maximilian:	I actually started out as a secretary. I couldn't find any internships in my city, but there were tons of positions for clerical help at the local ad agencies. I had taken a typing class in high school (I type 90 wpm), so I was a natural. And the female ad execs loved the idea of a male secretary! <g>
Thom H:	You've given me some great ideas, Max. Where do you work now, and would I know any of the campaigns you've worked on?
Maximilian:	I work for Miller & Morris Advertising. Have you seen the Monster Brewery campaign? I was the creative director on that. I also write all the copy for the Olivia's Boutique catalogs.
ThomH:	Hey that's cool! I loved the Monster Brewery ads—quite hip. And the Olivia's Boutique catalogs are sooo sexy. How do you keep from getting uh... you-know-what during the photo shoots? <g>
Maximilian:	Who says I don't? <weg>
DonA(Mod):	OK guys, better knock it off. This is a family forum, remember?
BevJ:	You're right, Don. In fact I think Maximilian is still going through puberty. <g,d&r>
Maximilian:	What do you mean—puberty? I'm already working on my mid-life crisis. <g>

DonA(Mod):	We need to get back on topic, here gang.
ThomH:	Maximilian, thanks again. I'll let you know how my interviews go.
Maximilian:	For your own sake, I hope you don't get a job at an ad agency. Get a nice career—selling insurance would be good. Or maybe you could be an editor, like Bev. <g> Well folks, gotta run. There's a martini chilling in my refrigerator and it's calling my name.
ThomH:	Bye Maximilian
KT:	Goodnight, Maximilian
BevJ:	Bye Maximilian
Maximilian:	Ciao everyone!
%System%:	Maximilian has left the forum.
ThomH:	Has anyone here actually met Maximilian?
KT:	Why do you ask, Thom?
ThomH:	Just wondering if he really did write that ad campaign.
KT:	He's for real. We were both panelists at a writer's convention a few years ago. He's a lousy public speaker, but with looks like that, who needs to know how to talk? ;-)

session:

3
4 5
6 7
8
9 10

> Private Mail
> Date: Wednesday, August 2, 1995 8:03 a.m.
> From: BevJ@frederic_gerard.com
> Subj: First Kiss
> To: Maximilian@miller&morris.com

My first kiss was pretty gross. I was twelve years old, and I was on one of my first dates with a boy named Bill Jablonski. He took me to our town's annual spring/summer carnival, called the "Tulip Festival." I had a huge crush on him, and I just *knew* that he would try to kiss me goodnight at the end of our date. In fact, that's all I could think about the whole night, so I really don't remember much of the evening except for what happened right before he kissed me goodnight.

He wanted me to go on the ferris wheel with him, but I was afraid of carnival rides (yes, even something as mild as a ferris wheel). So he went on it by himself while I stood on the ground and looked up at him and smiled and waved. I think he was a little ticked at me, but unfortunately he wasn't ticked off enough to change his mind about kissing me goodnight. The reason I say "unfortunately" is because Bill threw up in the bushes right after he got off the ferris wheel.

I was pretty mortified, but became even more so when I realized he still intended to give me a kiss goodnight. I mean, it wasn't like he had a toothbrush and a tube of toothpaste in his back pocket. I actually thought I was safe for a minute when we saw his dad's car pull into the parking lot, but Bill nailed me right before we started walking toward his dad's car.

Bill was my second boyfriend. My first boyfriend broke up with me because I wouldn't let him kiss me—I only wanted to hold hands. After The Bill Experience, it took two more boyfriends before I would even consider the idea of kissing again. By that time I was fourteen years old and was going steady with Kurt Aurelio, who provided me with a whole new perspective on kissing...<g>

Satisfied?

> Private Mail
> Date: Wednesday, August 2, 1995 9:47 a.m.
> From: Maximilian@miller&morris.com
> Subj: First Kiss
> To: BevJ@frederic_gerard.com

Are you still afraid to go on the ferris wheel?

> Private Mail
> Date: Thursday, August 3, 1995 7:08 a.m.
> From: BevJ@frederic_gerard.com
> Subj: First Kiss
> To: Maximilian@miller&morris.com

No—I like ferris wheel rides now. But I still won't go on the tilt-a-whirl.

Can we talk about something else now? <g>

> Private Mail
> Date: Thursday, August 3, 1995 10:51 a.m.
> From: Maximilian@miller&morris.com
> Subj: You
> To: BevJ@frederic_gerard.com

OK. Tell me what you look like.

> Private Mail
> Date: Friday, August 4, 1995 6:11 a.m.
> From: BevJ@frederic_gerard.com
> Subj: You
> To: Maximilian@miller&morris.com

Absolutely not. In fact, you're starting to piss me off
again, Maximilian. I have a husband, remember?

> Private Mail
> Date: Friday, August 4, 1995 4:19 p.m.
> From: Maximilian@miller&morris.com
> Subj: You
> To: BevJ@frederic_gerard.com

OK. Tell me what your husband looks like. <g>

> Private Mail
> Date: Monday, August 7, 1995 6:32 a.m.
> From: BevJ@frederic_gerard.com
> Subj: You
> To: Maximilian@miller&morris.com

Very funny. Let's talk about something normal, like,
where did you grow up?

> Private Mail
> Date: Tuesday, August 8, 1995 11:05 a.m.
> From: Maximilian@miller&morris.com
> Subj: You
> To: BevJ@frederic_gerard.com

Oh, you mean let's talk about something *safe*? All right...

Let's see, I was born in a suburb of Milwaukee. My dad was an actuary so we had a decent amount of money. My mom stayed at home and took care of me and my two sisters until we all went to college. My childhood was normal to the point of being boring.

Is it my turn to ask a question yet?

> Private Mail
> Date: Wednesday, August 9, 1995 6:32 a.m.
> From: BevJ@frederic_gerard.com
> Subj: You
> To: Maximilian@miller&morris.com

GA (not guaranteeing I'll answer it, however).

> Private Mail
> Date: Wednesday, August 9, 1995 9:30 a.m.
> From: Maximilian@miller&morris.com
> Subj: You
> To: BevJ@frederic_gerard.com

Why are you talking to me?

> Private Mail
> Date: Thursday, August 10, 1995 8:46 a.m.
> From: BevJ@frederic_gerard.com
> Subj: You
> To: Maximilian@miller&morris.com

I don't know.

> Private Mail
> Date: Thursday, August 10, 1995 9:14 a.m.
> From: Maximilian@miller&morris.com
> Subj: You
> To: BevJ@frederic_gerard.com

Bullshit.

I admit we don't know each other very well yet,
Beverly, but I do know enough about you to know
that you're not the type of person who does things
without a reason. So fess up. Why are you talking to
me?

> Private Mail
> Date: Thursday, August 10, 1995 5:37 p.m.
> From: BevJ@frederic_gerard.com
> Subj: Silly Me
> To: Maximilian@miller&morris.com

You've pretty much answered your own question, Maximilian. I'm talking to you because I don't have a reason for talking to you.

Beverly

> Private Mail
> Date: Thursday, August 10, 1995 8:57 p.m.
> From: Maximilian@miller&morris.com
> Subj: Silly Me
> To: BevJ@frederic_gerard.com

What? ::: shaking head :::

I don't understand.

> Private Mail
> Date: Friday, August 11, 1995 8:42 a.m.
> From: BevJ@frederic_gerard.com
> Subj: Silly Me
> To: Maximilian@miller&morris.com

You're right in saying that I'm the kind of person
who does everything for a reason. I've worked hard
to get my life the way I want it, and I'm proud of
that. But sometimes I feel like doing something
that's just a little bit irrational. Talking to a stranger
like this online is something I just wouldn't normally
do.

> Private Mail
> Date: Friday, August 11, 1995 10:01 a.m.
> From: Maximilian@miller&morris.com
> Subj: Silly Me
> To: BevJ@frederic_gerard.com

So why am I different?

> Private Mail
> Date: Friday, August 11, 1995 4:20 p.m.
> From: BevJ@frederic_gerard.com
> Subj: Silly Me
> To: Maximilian@miller&morris.com

I haven't figured that out yet.

session: 1 2 3 4 **5** 6 7 8

> Private Mail
> Date: Saturday, August 12, 1995 3:18 a.m.
> From: Maximilian@miller&morris.com
> Subj: Macworld
> To: BevJ@frederic_gerard.com

Beverly,

I heard about this computer trade show called
Macworld that's being held in Boston later this
month, and I was wondering if you go to those sorts
of things. Believe it or not, I wasn't making it up
when I first wrote to you and told you I was looking
for a new computer. So I've been thinking about
going to this trade show and maybe buying a Mac

while I'm there. I've also heard there are some pretty happenin' parties at these shows. <g>

> Private Mail
> Date: Monday, August 14, 1995 10:22 a.m.
> From: BevJ@frederic_gerard.com
> Subj: Macworld
> To: Maximilian@miller&morris.com

Maximilian:

First of all, if you do decide to go to Macworld, DO NOT, I repeat, DO NOT buy your computer there. It would be much better if you go through your local dealer. That way, you can also get tech support and perhaps a better warranty. Having said that, and if you've made up your mind that you want a Macintosh rather than a PC, it's still a good idea for you to go to a show like Macworld. You can hear about the latest technology, check out all the new hardware and software for yourself on the trade show floor, and hear a lot of experts give their not-so-humble opinions.

And some of the parties are pretty good, too. ;-)

Beverly

> Private Mail
> Date: Monday, August 14, 1995 10:40 a.m.
> From: Maximilian@miller&morris.com
> Subj: Macworld
> To: BevJ@frederic_gerard.com

Oh, so you *do* go to these types of shows? Will you
be going to this one?

> Private Mail
> Date: Tuesday, August 15, 1995 8:59 a.m.
> From: BevJ@frederic_gerard.com
> Subj: Macworld
> To: Maximilian@miller&morris.com

No, I won't be going. Actually, this is one of the
shows I usually go to because a few of my authors
sell lots of their computer books there, but I won't
be able to make it this time. I have another big
deadline coming up, and though I'd love to get away,
I just can't. Besides, the show is coming up here
pretty quickly—it's in a couple of weeks, isn't it?

How about you? Are you going to go?

> Private Mail
> Date: Tuesday, August 15, 1995 9:28 a.m.
> From: Maximilian@miller&morris.com
> Subj: Macworld
> To: BevJ@frederic_gerard.com

Oh, too bad. I was hoping we could jump each
other's bones or something. <g,d&r>

> Private Mail
> Date: Wednesday, August 16, 1995 7:32 a.m.
> From: BevJ@frederic_gerard.com
> Subj: Get Real
> To: Maximilian@miller&morris.com

Maximilian:

For Chrissakes, I tell you a few personal things about
myself and now you think I'm going to hop in the
sack with you?

I knew I shouldn't have continued talking with you...
<sigh>

Beverly

p.s. And besides, I thought you said I was probably a
real toad?

> Private Mail
> Date: Wednesday, August 16, 1995 11:29 a.m.
> From: Maximilian@miller&morris.com
> Subj: Get Real
> To: BevJ@frederic_gerard.com

Sorry. I knew you were going to get upset with me when I wrote that. I'm a guy—sometimes I just can't help myself. <sheepish grin>

Friends?

p.s. I'd still want to talk to you, even if you are a toad.

> Private Mail
> Date: Thursday, August 17, 1995 6:43 a.m.
> From: BevJ@frederic_gerard.com
> Subj: Get Real
> To: Maximilian@miller&morris.com

Oh gee, how charitable of you—you mean you actually talk to ugly girls too? I am *soooo* impressed. What a big man you must be.

Beverly

> Private Mail
> Date: Thursday, August 17, 1995 10:42 a.m.
> From: Maximilian@miller&morris.com
> Subj: Get Real
> To: BevJ@frederic_gerard.com

Come on, Bev. I'm sorry. And I wasn't making a joke
when I said I'd still want to talk with you, no matter
what you look like. You know, you piss me off sometimes too.

> Private Mail
> Date: Thursday, August 17, 1995 12:30 p.m.
> From: BevJ@frederic_gerard.com
> Subj: Get Real
> To: Maximilian@miller&morris.com

And why is that?

> Private Mail
> Date: Thursday, August 17, 1995 1:44 p.m.
> From: Maximilian@miller&morris.com
> Subj: Get Real
> To: BevJ@frederic_gerard.com

Because you intrigue the hell out of me.

> Private Mail
> Date: Thursday, August 17, 1995 3:38 p.m.
> From: BevJ@frederic_gerard.com
> Subj: Game?
> To: Maximilian@miller&morris.com

Maximilian:

I find that hard to believe. Since we've started "talking" to each other, I've told you more about myself
than you've told me about yourself.

I have an idea. How about if we play a little game?

> Private Mail
> Date: Friday, August 18, 1995 1:00 a.m.
> From: Maximilian@miller&morris.com
> Subj: Game?
> To: BevJ@frederic_gerard.com

A little game of virtual strip poker perhaps?

JUST KIDDING!!!

Seriously, what kind of game do you want to play?

> Private Mail
> Date: Friday, August 18, 1995 7:53 a.m.
> From: BevJ@frederic_gerard.com
> Subj: Game?
> To: Maximilian@miller&morris.com

Tell me something you've never told anyone else before.

> Private Mail
> Date: Friday, August 18, 1995 9:24 a.m.
> From: Maximilian@miller&morris.com
> Subj: Game?
> To: BevJ@frederic_gerard.com

Seriously?

> Private Mail
> Date: Friday, August 18, 1995 4:56 p.m.
> From: BevJ@frederic_gerard.com
> Subj: Game?
> To: Maximilian@miller&morris.com

Seriously.

> Private Mail
> Date: Saturday, August 19, 1995 2:55 a.m.
> From: Maximilian@miller&morris.com
> Subj: Game?
> To: BevJ@frederic_gerard.com

OK. Here goes. ::: taking deep breath :::

I've never been in love.

session:

6 7 8

1
2 3
4
9 1

> Private Mail
> Date: Sunday, August 20, 1995 12:59 a.m.
> From: Maximilian@miller&morris.com
> Subj: Shit!
> To: BevJ@frederic_gerard.com

Beverly,

I can't believe I sent you that message last night. I'm feeling like a real dork right now.

Can I retract it?

Maximilian

> Private Mail
> Date: Monday, August 21, 1995 5:29 a.m.
> From: BevJ@frederic_gerard.com
> Subj: Shit!
> To: Maximilian@miller&morris.com

Maximilian:

No, you can't retract the message—unless you've fallen in love overnight—and no, I don't think you're a dork.

I do admit to feeling somewhat speechless in response to your message. I'm not quite sure what to say. (When in doubt, pretend you're a therapist: "So, Max, how does that make you feel?") <g>

Don't mean to make light of things, but I guess I do want to know if this is something that weighs heavily on your heart.

Bev

> Private Mail
> Date: Monday, August 21, 1995 9:08 a.m.
> From: Maximilian@miller&morris.com
> Subj: Shit!
> To: BevJ@frederic_gerard.com

Bev,

I'm glad you don't think I'm some sort of major domo dork. Sometimes I think I must be if I've never fallen in love before.

It's not as if I haven't been involved in more than my share of serious relationships (and some not-so-serious ones too). I was even engaged once, and broke off the relationship about six weeks before the wedding (yes, right after the invitations went out—what a jerk I am).

I've never even said "I love you" to anyone but my parents—not even to my fiancée. One of the reasons I called off the wedding was that it finally occurred to me how strange it was that she still wanted to marry me, even though I never told her I loved her. Turns out she had her own set of issues, as Tracy recently told me that she has fallen in love with her best friend (a woman) and has never been happier. I'm happy for her too, but that doesn't solve my own little mystery.

Sometimes I wonder if maybe I have been in love before but was just too stupid to recognize it. I guess it *is* something that weighs heavily on my heart, because I feel as if I'm missing out on something.

What does it feel like to be in love?

Max

> Private Mail
> Date: Tuesday, August 22, 1995 8:37 a.m.
> From: BevJ@frederic_gerard.com
> Subj: Luv
> To: Maximilian@miller&morris.com

Max:

I suppose it's different for everyone. For a lot of
people, I imagine falling in love is just like it's
described in popular novels—an adrenaline rush, like
walking on air, with your head in the clouds—all
that happy horseshit. For others, I imagine falling in
love is more painful—angst, longing, and heartache.

I admire the fact that you've never lied and told anyone you loved them when you didn't (and I'm sure
you must have been tempted). On more than one
occasion I've said "I love you" when I knew damn
well I didn't. I'm not sure why I did it, because I
consider myself an honest person. It was probably to
avoid an uncomfortable moment, or just to get some
gorgeous hunk in the sack. <g>

For me, falling in love has always been a mixture of
electricity and calm. The electricity having to do
with the chemistry and the sexual attraction, of
course, and the calmness comes from a feeling of ful-
fillment and peace.

Bev

> Private Mail
> Date: Tuesday, August 22, 1995 11:47 a.m.
> From: Maximilian@miller&morris.com
> Subj: Luv
> To: BevJ@frederic_gerard.com

So you've been in love more than once?

> Private Mail
> Date: Wednesday, August 23, 1995 7:28 a.m.
> From: BevJ@frederic_gerard.com
> Subj: Luv
> To: Maximilian@miller&morris.com

Yes.

> Private Mail
> Date: Wednesday, August 23, 1995 9:06 a.m.
> From: Maximilian@miller&morris.com
> Subj: Luv
> To: BevJ@frederic_gerard.com

Do you love your husband?

> Private Mail
> Date: Wednesday, August 23, 1995 5:51 p.m.
> From: BevJ@frederic_gerard.com
> Subj: Luv
> To: Maximilian@miller&morris.com

Yes.

> Tuesday August 29, 1995 7:07 p.m.

> Writer's Forum   > Live Conference   > People Here: 11

DonA(Mod): Hello everyone. The topic of tonight's
live CO is our semi-annual Macworld
update, in which our forum members
who were lucky enough to attend the
show fill us in on all the hot technology news, especially any news that's per-
tinent to the Writer's Forum. Our spe-
cial guest tonight is Beverly Johnson,
editor-in-chief of Frederic Gerard
books, who attended the show in
Boston just this past weekend. Let's let

	Bev tell us about all the interesting things she saw, and then we'll open up the floor to questions.
	Bev?
BevJ:	Thanks, Don, and hello everyone. Probably the biggest excitement at the show was over the new Power Macs—Apple's booth was literally mobbed with people trying to get a peek at the new models. Storage devices were another hot item at the show—as were authoring tools for the WWW.
BruceF:	?
DonA(Mod):	GA, Bruce.
BruceF:	Did you go to any good parties?
BevJ:	Yeah, the Fractal party was wild!
Kass:	?
DonA(Mod):	GA, Kass.
Kass:	Did you see the new Web layout application called PageMill?
BevJ:	Yep—it was a big hit at the show. Guy Kawasaki called it "the PageMaker of the '90s."
Maximilian:	?
DonA(Mod):	GA Maximilian.
Maximilian:	I thought you said you weren't going to be at Macworld, Bev?
BevJ:	I thought I wasn't going to go, but my publisher sent me at the last minute. Did you go?
Maximilian:	Yeah! It was great. I can't believe you didn't let me know you were going to be there.

BevJ:	I thought about trying to contact you, but I didn't bring my PowerBook so I had no way of sending e-mail.
DonA(Mod):	Ahem. Excuse me guys, can we get back on track here?
Maximilian:	Oh, sure Don. Sorry. <g>
BevJ:	Sorry Don! Does anyone else have any questions?
Nightwrtr:	?
DonA(Mod):	GA, Nightwrtr—you're new to the forum, aren't you? Go ahead and introduce yourself to the rest of the group if you'd like.
Nightwrtr:	I just want to know what color underwear Bev is wearing.
BevJ:	Uh, Don, can you get rid of this guy?
DonA(Mod):	Just a sec...hold on everyone...AFK
%System%:	Nightwrtr has left the forum.
Kass:	What a creep.
BevJ:	Whew!
	::: going to the fridge to get a beer :::
%System%:	Maximilian has left the forum.

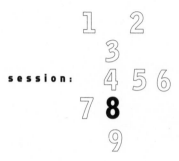

session:

1 2
3 4 5 6
7 **8**
9

> Private Mail
> Date: Wednesday, August 30, 1995 1:40 a.m.
> From: Maximilian@miller&morris.com
> Subj: Fine, Blow Me Off
> To: BevJ@frederic_gerard.com

Beverly,

I can't believe you didn't try to contact me before
you left for Macworld. In fact, I'm sort of pissed. I
thought we were developing a friendship here, or is
there some sort of cyber etiquette that says you're
not supposed to meet the people you correspond with
online?

Maximilian

> Private Mail
> Date: Wednesday, August 30, 1995 7:46 a.m.
> From: BevJ@frederic_gerard.com
> Subj: Fine, Blow Me Off
> To: Maximilian@miller&morris.com

I guess you really are mad at me, since you've gone back to calling me Beverly instead of Bev. <g>

> Private Mail
> Date: Wednesday, August 30, 1995 9:12 a.m.
> From: Maximilian@miller&morris.com
> Subj: Fine, Blow Me Off
> To: BevJ@frederic_gerard.com

Now who's being a smart-ass?

Come on, is there a reason you didn't try to contact me?

> Private Mail
> Date: Thursday, August 31, 1995 8:37 a.m.
> From: BevJ@frederic_gerard.com
> Subj: Fine, Blow Me Off
> To: Maximilian@miller&morris.com

Max:

Part of the reason I didn't contact you was that I

didn't have time—honest. I got your last message right before I found out I had to leave town. I immediately left the office to go home and pack, and I caught my flight to Boston that night.

Bev

> Private Mail
> Date: Thursday, August 31, 1995 9:56 a.m.
> From: Maximilian@miller&morris.com
> Subj: Fine, Blow Me Off
> To: BevJ@frederic_gerard.com

Hmmmm. So you had to fly to Boston? I guess that means you don't live there, or at least you don't live within driving distance.

> Private Mail
> Date: Friday, September 1, 1995 9:01 a.m.
> From: BevJ@frederic_gerard.com
> Subj: Fine, Blow Me Off
> To: Maximilian@miller&morris.com

Maximilian, it says in my member profile I live in the Midwest, remember? (And no, I'm not going to tell you any more than that.)

> Private Mail
> Date: Friday, September 1, 1995 11:58 a.m.
> From: Maximilian@miller&morris.com
> Subj: Fine, Blow Me Off
> To: BevJ@frederic_gerard.com

So what's the other part of the reason you didn't try
to get in touch with me?

> Private Mail
> Date: Monday, September 4, 1995 12:01 a.m.
> From: Maximilian@miller&morris.com
> Subj: Fine, Blow Me Off
> To: BevJ@frederic_gerard.com

Hello? Bev? Are you there?

Max

> Private Mail
> Date: Tuesday, September 5, 1995 10:00 a.m.
> From: BevJ@frederic_gerard.com
> Subj: Fine, Blow Me Off
> To: Maximilian@miller&morris.com

Max:

I'm sorry I didn't write back to you sooner—it was
Labor Day weekend, and we went away for a few

days. Besides, even though I do have a computer and modem at home, I usually only log on from the office.

If you must know, the other reason I didn't try to contact you before I left for Macworld is because I was afraid to.

Bev

> Private Mail
> Date: Tuesday, September 5, 1995 1:23 p.m.
> From: Maximilian@miller&morris.com
> Subj: Fine, Blow Me Off
> To: BevJ@frederic_gerard.com

You've got to be kidding. Why would you be afraid to meet me in person?

Max

> Private Mail
> Date: Wednesday, September 6, 1995 6:06 a.m.
> From: BevJ@frederic_gerard.com
> Subj: Fine, Blow Me Off
> To: Maximilian@miller&morris.com

Because I was afraid of what might happen between us.

> Private Mail
> Date: Wednesday, September 6, 1995 8:58 a.m.
> From: Maximilian@miller&morris.com
> Subj: Fine, Blow Me Off
> To: BevJ@frederic_gerard.com

You mean you actually *would* let me jump your
bones?! Hot damn! This is what I call progress!
<g,d&r>

> Private Mail
> Date: Thursday, September 7, 1995 8:11 a.m.
> From: BevJ@frederic_gerard.com
> Subj: Fine, Blow Me Off
> To: Maximilian@miller&morris.com

Sometimes I wonder why I continue talking with
you.

There are a lot of things that could go wrong if we
were to meet each other in person, and yes, I admit
that I feel a certain attraction toward you and one of
the reasons I was afraid to get together was that that
attraction might lead to something complicated.

But what's more likely to happen when two people
who have been corresponding online meet each other
in person is that the whole thing is extremely anti-
climactic and both people end up being disappointed
or hurt. Even if the two people are just friends
online and they meet as friends in person, the reality

of the situation is that the chemistry is usually wildly different (or nonexistent) from any kind of chemistry that may have been happening online. And what's worse, once the two people have met each other F2F (that's face-to-face) and they try to return to their online relationship, the magic has disappeared.

I've seen it happen a dozen times throughout the years, Maximilian. Two people get all hot and bothered over an online romance that goes on for months, and then they meet somewhere and it's all just very awkward and uncomfortable. The same thing can happen even when two people are just friends. There was one woman I developed quite a friendship with over a period of time through our professional affiliation and correspondence online, but when I finally met her for lunch in an airport on my way through her town, she totally grated on my nerves.

I mean, it wasn't this woman's looks or anything about her physical appearance that caught me off guard. It was just that what seemed benign in cyberspace was totally annoying in real life. Through our e-mail correspondence, I knew she was somewhat pushy and a little bit on the zany side. But in person, her behavior seemed inappropriate. I was embarrassed by how rude she was to our waitress. And before I even finished eating, she lit up a cigarette and tapped the ashes onto the remains of her club sandwich. Those things by themselves weren't really major, but she didn't even seem genuinely interested in anything I had to say—she just rambled about herself and her business the whole time and the fact that I was even there seemed completely secondary to her. When we resumed our online correspondence, I couldn't stop thinking of her boorish little habits. The friendship was never the same after that.

Granted, there are success stories of people who have met online. One woman I know met her husband here; they now are happily married, have two beautiful little girls, and I'm sure they will have a long and fulfilling life together. There are several people I know who have had enjoyable flings with people they met online, and as for myself, I have made dozens of friends here whom I've met at trade shows and who are still an extremely positive influence on my life.

But when it comes to me and you, I just don't want to take the chance. I don't want to lose your friendship, Maximilian.

Beverly

> Private Mail
> Date: Thursday, September 7, 1995 10:42 a.m.
> From: Maximilian@miller&morris.com
> Subj: Fine, Blow Me Off
> To: BevJ@frederic_gerard.com

I think I can understand that. On to lighter topics.

Did you have a good time at Macworld?

> Private Mail
> Date: Friday, September 8, 1995 7:26 a.m.
> From: BevJ@frederic_gerard.com
> Subj: Macworld & Stuff
> To: Maximilian@miller&morris.com

Maximilian:

Yeah, I had a good time at Macworld. It was...interesting.

How about you? Did you have fun? Did you decide which Mac you're going to buy?

And btw, how's everything going with your job? Is the situation with your boss getting any better?

> Private Mail
> Date: Friday, September 8, 1995 9:35 p.m.
> From: Maximilian@miller&morris.com
> Subj: Macworld & Stuff
> To: BevJ@frederic_gerard.com

I had a great time—what a fun show! I even made the rounds of the parties. As for which computer I'm going to buy, I'm still deciding between one of the new PowerBooks and a full-blown Power Mac. I like the idea of having a portable computer, so I'm leaning toward the PowerBook, but I don't do all that much traveling, so then I think I should get a Power Mac (really decisive here). <g>

My boss is still a psychopath. What's worse, some wacko millionaire has decided to sue my agency for trademark infringement over an ad campaign that *I* wrote. Now my boss has taken me off the account (it was a plum, too) and I'm in the shithouse because the agency is hemorrhaging money trying to defend itself in this stupid lawsuit. The guy who's suing us doesn't have a leg to stand on, but the agency still has to pay a wild pack of attorneys to settle the damn thing.

I'm thinking about changing careers. I think I wouldn't even try to go to a different agency; they're all nuthouses. A friend of mine who is an account exec at one of the other big agencies here in town just lost his job last week—I guess the creative direc-tor and a bunch of other key players decided to jump ship and form their own agency, so half the accounts followed them. My friend's agency is now "downsizing" and he got laid off with not even a severance package, just his last paycheck and a "don't let the door hit you in the ass on your way out."

Sorry for the flame-let. (Is that what you would call a minor flame?) <g>

Thanks for letting me blow off some steam. I'm actually trying not to let the whole thing get me too depressed—putting things in perspective and all that. After all, it's just a friggin' job, right?

Max

> Private Mail
> Date: Monday, September 11, 1995 6:52 a.m.
> From: BevJ@frederic_gerard.com
> Subj: Ideal Job
> To: Maximilian@miller&morris.com

How right you are, Maximilian. I guess I'm pretty lucky in that I'm finally happy with my job situation. I worked for a string of jerks early in my career, and somehow I seemed to have found a place that allows me to do the best job that I can with a minimum amount of bullshit.

What would be your ideal career?

> Private Mail
> Date: Monday, September 11, 1995 8:14 a.m.
> From: Maximilian@miller&morris.com
> Subj: Ideal Job
> To: BevJ@frederic_gerard.com

I don't know. When I was a kid I wanted to be a professional hockey player. I was captain of my high school and college hockey teams, and we won all sorts of championships and I was pretty much a big stud. There was this kid on my high school hockey team who was smaller than everyone else, and we used to give him so much shit, like stuffing him in his hockey bag and things like that. Now he plays for the Chicago Blackhawks and is one of the highest paid players in the NHL.

I guess that goes to show that things aren't always what they appear to be.

Now that I'm a grown-up, I think my ideal career would be working as a UPS delivery man. They get to drive those big brown trucks all over town, wear shorts to work in the summertime, and, if they get the right route, they can deliver packages to all those women who work from home and answer their doors in various stages of undress. <g>

I guess since you already have the ideal job, I can't ask you what yours would be. Geez, perfect husband, perfect job, perfect life...what more could a girl want?

> Private Mail
> Date: Tuesday, September 12, 1995 9:07 a.m.
> From: BevJ@frederic_gerard.com
> Subj: Ideal Job
> To: Maximilian@miller&morris.com

Oh, Maximilian. You know, I hate it when people say things like that. As you just said, things aren't always what they appear to be.

session: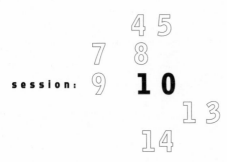

> Private Mail
> Date: Wednesday, September 13, 1995 8:09 a.m.
> From: BevJ@frederic_gerard.com
> Subj: Getting To Know You
> To: Maximilian@miller&morris.com

Maximilian:

I was wondering—what kinds of things do you do in
your free time? I notice you log on a lot late at night
during the weekends. Your member profile says you
write poetry and do bonsai gardening. Do you really
do that?

Also, how can you drink martinis? Those things are
gross! <g>

> Private Mail
> Date: Wednesday, September 13, 1995 11:41 a.m.
> From: Maximilian@miller&morris.com
> Subj: Getting To Know You
> To: BevJ@frederic_gerard.com

Bev,

I love martinis—been drinking 'em since I was
twelve. (Just kidding!) You should hear me order a
martini in a restaurant. It takes me several minutes
to explain to the waitress exactly how I want it: dry
martini on the rocks—make that a *very* dry martini
on the rocks, in fact, just wave the bottle of ver-
mouth somewhere in the vicinity of the glass—not
too many rocks, make sure the glass is chilled, with
four anchovy olives. Don't have anchovy olives?
Forget it! <g>

That's why I like going to my regular hangouts; they
know exactly how to fix my martinis without my having to explain everything to them. I like getting the
extra olives because then I feel like I've had something solid to eat with my drink. And I figure with
the anchovies, I'm getting another one of the four
food groups.

I used to write a lot of poetry, but I haven't had time
to write as much as I used to (too busy dreaming up
snappy headlines I guess). I still do bonsai gardening, though. I've got five bonsai trees out on my bal-
cony right now; one of them is eleven years old—it's
a beaut.

Other than that, I do a lot of regular guy stuff: hang out with my friends, watch hockey on TV, and cruise the information superhighway. (And yes, I do log on late at night—I'm a night owl, and am usually awake until two or three in the morning.)

How about you? Do you really study typography in your spare time, or did you just put that in your member profile to make you look more like an intellectual? <g>

Max

> Private Mail
> Date: Thursday, September 14, 1995 5:15 a.m.
> From: BevJ@frederic_gerard.com
> Subj: Getting To Know You
> To: Maximilian@miller&morris.com

Yes, I really do study typography in my spare time. My home office is loaded with books on type, though I'm still pretty much a novice. My goal is to someday be able to recognize typefaces just by looking at them. As it is now, I usually have to go through my type specimen books in order to match a typeface to its name. Once in a while I'll recognize a typeface on a billboard as we're driving down the street, and get all excited about it. My husband thinks that's pretty funny.

My favorite leisure-time activity is reading, however.

I'm your average bookworm—always have my nose in something, with two or three unfinished novels on my night stand at any point in time. I like reading biographies, mysteries, self-help books, and I'll even admit to reading computer books on occasion. I used to play the piano a lot (I studied classical piano as a kid), but I'm not as good as I used to be, and that bothers me. Someday I'd like to study jazz piano and get a job doing a lounge act where I can wear sequined evening gowns and long black gloves to work. <g>

And I suppose I'd better tell you here and now that I'm a beer-drinking kind of gal. <g> I've never liked mixed drinks (especially martinis—yick!), but I do enjoy an occasional beer with dinner. (And not the wimpy stuff either—I like brown ales, stouts, and porters.)

> Private Mail
> Date: Thursday, September 14, 1995 10:04 a.m.
> From: Maximilian@miller&morris.com
> Subj: Getting To Know You
> To: BevJ@frederic_gerard.com

Hmmm. I've only met one other woman who likes to drink the heavier beers. Myself, I prefer a drink that contains less foam and more alcohol. <g>

Self-help books? Why do you read self-help books? I

mean, you just don't seem like the type…I guess I
think of you as more together than that.

> Private Mail
> Date: Friday, September 15, 1995 5:36 a.m.
> From: BevJ@frederic_gerard.com
> Subj: Getting To Know You
> To: Maximilian@miller&morris.com

Well, it's not something I would tell most people. I
actually don't read as many as I used to—in fact I
think I overdosed on them during one period of my
life, and a lot of the books I read were pretty use-
less—but I think they do serve a purpose for some
people. Most of the books I've read have to do with
positive thinking and stuff like that.

Can we change the subject? <g>

> Private Mail
> Date: Friday, September 15, 1995 11:22 a.m.
> From: Maximilian@miller&morris.com
> Subj: Getting to Know *All* About You
> To: BevJ@frederic_gerard.com

OK. I have an idea…

> Private Mail
> Date: Monday, September 18, 1995 8:13 a.m.
> From: BevJ@frederic_gerard.com
> Subj: Getting To Know *All* About You
> To: Maximilian@miller&morris.com

Oh, God! You're having a brainstorm! Does it hurt?
<g>

(And from the way you changed the subject in the
message header, something tells me I'm not going to
like this idea...)

> Private Mail
> Date: Monday, September 18, 1995 9:40 a.m.
> From: Maximilian@miller&morris.com
> Subj: Getting To Know *All* About You
> To: BevJ@frederic_gerard.com

My, my, aren't you the little comedienne. <g>

> Private Mail
> Date: Tuesday, September 19, 1995 5:53 a.m.
> From: BevJ@frederic_gerard.com
> Subj: Getting To Know *All* About You
> To: Maximilian@miller&morris.com

So what's your brilliant idea, Einstein?

> Private Mail
> Date: Tuesday, September 19, 1995 10:16 a.m.
> From: Maximilian@miller&morris.com
> Subj: Getting To Know *All* About You
> To: BevJ@frederic_gerard.com

I want you to tell me something you've never told
anyone else before.

> Private Mail
> Date: Wednesday, September 20, 1995 7:02 a.m.
> From: BevJ@frederic_gerard.com
> Subj: Getting To Know *All* About You
> To: Maximilian@miller&morris.com

Aw, for cryin' out loud! Can't you think of something
more original? That was my idea!

> Private Mail
> Date: Wednesday, September 20, 1995 10:36 a.m.
> From: Maximilian@miller&morris.com
> Subj: Getting To Know *All* About You
> To: BevJ@frederic_gerard.com

So sue me. Are you going to answer my question or
not? I answered yours—turnabout's fair play, isn't it?

> Private Mail
> Date: Thursday, September 21, 1995 7:45 a.m.
> From: BevJ@frederic_gerard.com
> Subj: Getting To Know *All* About You
> To: Maximilian@miller&morris.com

Can I think about it for a few days?

> Private Mail
> Date: Thursday, September 21, 1995 10:18 a.m.
> From: Maximilian@miller&morris.com
> Subj: Getting To Know *All* About You
> To: BevJ@frederic_gerard.com

I guess I have no choice but to wait.

> Private Mail
> Date: Monday, September 25, 1995 7:17 a.m.
> From: BevJ@frederic_gerard.com
> Subj: Getting To Know *All* About You
> To: Maximilian@miller&morris.com

Max:

OK, I've mulled it over all weekend, and have decided to give you your damn answer. This is something I have honestly not told anyone and I can't believe I'm about to spill my guts to you, but...

I've had an affair.

Now I suppose whatever respect you may have had
for me is completely lost.

session: **11**

> Private Mail
> Date: Thursday, September 28, 1995 4:57 a.m.
> From: BevJ@frederic_gerard.com
> Subj: Hello?
> To: Maximilian@miller&morris.com

Maximilian:

I knew it—you're upset with me; you hate me; you think I'm a big flake. I haven't gotten a response from you in four days and your silence is killing me.

Bev

> Private Mail
> Date: Friday, September 29, 1995 5:03 a.m.
> From: BevJ@frederic_gerard.com
> Subj: Hello?
> To: Maximilian@miller&morris.com

Maximilian? Are you there? Please answer this message. Even if you want to say something mean to me, just say something, OK?

Bev

> Private Mail
> Date: Friday, September 29, 1995 11:44 p.m.
> From: Maximilian@miller&morris.com
> Subj: Hello?
> To: BevJ@frederic_gerard.com

Bev,

I can't believe you did that! What about your husband? I thought you guys were happily married, so why the hell did you go and do something stupid like have an affair?

Max

> Private Mail
> Date: Saturday, September 30, 1995 9:12 a.m.
> From: BevJ@frederic_gerard.com
> Subj: Hello?
> To: Maximilian@miller&morris.com

Maximilian:

I can't believe you're berating me for having an affair
when you've been trying to pick me up online for
two months now.

Beverly

p.s. And besides, it wasn't exactly a full-blown affair.
It was more like a one-night stand.

> Private Mail
> Date: Sunday, October 1, 1995 3:14 a.m.
> From: Maximilian@miller&morris.com
> Subj: Hello?
> To: BevJ@frederic_gerard.com

A one-night stand?! Bev, how could you do that?! I
simply cannot believe it.

And I haven't exactly been trying to pick you up. I
mean, it's not as if I could jump through the modem
and put my hand on your knee or anything...

> Private Mail
> Date: Monday, October 2, 1995 8:18 a.m.
> From: BevJ@frederic_gerard.com
> Subj: Harmless?
> To: Maximilian@miller&morris.com

And I can't believe you're being so judgmental of me,
like you're Mr. Perfect or something. I just thought
you'd be a little more understanding.

> Private Mail
> Date: Monday, October 2, 1995 9:21 a.m.
> From: Maximilian@miller&morris.com
> Subj: Harmless?
> To: BevJ@frederic_gerard.com

Aww, I'm sorry. I suppose I'm a little taken aback. I
mean, you've really shifted my paradigm here. <g>

I guess I had you up on this pedestal, thinking you
were this perfect, untouchable sort of woman, and
I'm feeling a little pissed, and disappointed,
and...jealous.

> Private Mail
> Date: Tuesday, October 3, 1995 5:24 a.m.
> From: BevJ@frederic_gerard.com
> Subj: Harmless?
> To: Maximilian@miller&morris.com

Apology accepted. I'm feeling pretty disappointed in myself, too. It doesn't exactly fit in with my vision of who I'm supposed to be.

> Private Mail
> Date: Tuesday, October 3, 1995 9:39 a.m.
> From: Maximilian@miller&morris.com
> Subj: Harmless?
> To: BevJ@frederic_gerard.com

So who was this guy, anyway?

> Private Mail
> Date: Wednesday, October 4, 1995 8:25 a.m.
> From: BevJ@frederic_gerard.com
> Subj: Harmless?
> To: Maximilian@miller&morris.com

I don't know.

> Private Mail
> Date: Wednesday, October 4, 1995 10:47 a.m.
> From: Maximilian@miller&morris.com
> Subj: Harmless?
> To: BevJ@frederic_gerard.com

WHAT?!!! WHAT DO YOU MEAN, YOU DON'T KNOW ???

> Private Mail
> Date: Wednesday, October 4, 1995 1:06 p.m.
> From BevJ@frederic_gerard.com
> Subj: Harmless?
> To: Maximilian@miller&morris.com

Max,

Please quit shouting at me. I mean exactly what I said. I don't know who he is. I met him at a party.

Bev

> Private Mail
> Date: Wednesday, October 4, 1995 4:24 p.m.
> From: Maximilian@miller&morris.com
> Subj: Harmless?
> To: BevJ@frederic_gerard.com

OK. I'll quit shouting. But how could you meet a guy at a party, sleep with him, and not know who he is?

> Private Mail
> Date: Thursday, October 5, 1995 7:29 a.m.
> From: BevJ@frederic_gerard.com
> Subj: Harmless?
> To: Maximilian@miller&morris.com

I don't even know his first name.

> Private Mail
> Date: Thursday, October 5, 1995 9:31 a.m.
> From: Maximilian@miller&morris.com
> Subj: Fear of Flying
> To: BevJ@frederic_gerard.com

Oh, that's just great. Fucking great. So, what...you think you're Erica Jong or something?

> Private Mail
> Date: Friday, October 6, 1995 8:12 a.m.
> From: BevJ@frederic_gerard.com
> Subj: Fear of Flying
> To: Maximilian@miller&morris.com

Very funny, Maximilian. I didn't think you were the type who reads chick books (I like your message header, btw). <g>

> Private Mail
> Date: Friday, October 6, 1995 10:56 a.m.
> From: Maximilian@miller&morris.com
> Subj: Fear of Flying
> To: BevJ@frederic_gerard.com

Thanks, I thought it was rather clever myself. <g>

So, is there anything you *do* know about this guy?

> Private Mail
> Date: Saturday, October 7, 1995 9:50 a.m.
> From: BevJ@frederic_gerard.com
> Subj: Fear of Flying
> To: Maximilian@miller&morris.com

Well I guess that depends on what sorts of things you're talking about.

I don't know his name, where he lives, what he does for a living, how old he is, or anything concrete like that.

I do know that he was the most irresistable man I've ever encountered. I mean, I just couldn't help myself, Max. I'm really ashamed to say it, but it's true.

It was at Macworld—at the Fractal party in the Boston Computer Museum. I was there by myself and everybody there was doing the typical trade show routine: schmoozing, drinking wine out of clear plastic cups, nibbling on chunks of cheese, and pretending to be interested in the computer-generated artwork on the walls. I spotted him first—I think—and couldn't take my eyes off of him. I mean, really, it was embarrassing. But I didn't stop looking at him, admiring the cut of his charcoal gray suit, the fuschia and violet colors in his linen tie, his crisp white shirt (amazing how fresh it looked after a long day on the show floor), his long, curly black hair, strong nose (it was kind of big but added nicely to the whole effect), olive skin, green eyes, long lashes. He had this feminine-looking mouth; his entire appearance was a strange mix of seedy and cleancut.

It didn't take long for him to notice me staring at him—I was sure I was making a total ass of myself—but he smiled at me and then looked away. I can't explain what came over me but I just walked up to him; he saw me coming and smiled again. I said "hi" and he said "hi." Silence. Usually at this point people at these parties would start talking about who they worked for and what they were doing at the show. But he just began talking about this piece of artwork that we were standing in front of, and how much prettier it would have been if it had actually been done in watercolor instead of in a software program. So we talked like that for a long time, wandering around the museum, picking up glasses of wine from the waiters who walked around with the trays of plastic wine cups, and talking about all the interesting objects we came across.

At one point we realized that we were the only people left at the party and that the caterers were packing up. By this time I was completely crazed over this man, and I was sure he felt the same way about me. It was chemistry of the most basic sort.

We stepped outside to the taxi line and I asked him to come back to my room with me. I didn't even know his name. But he said he'd very much like to come back to the room with me, so there we were in the back seat of the taxi, on our way to my hotel. We weren't even holding hands or anything. But there was one hell of an electrical storm going on in the back of that taxi.

About halfway back to the hotel, it occurred to me that I didn't have any type of, um, protection. I became panic-stricken, but I don't think he noticed. When we arrived in front of my hotel, I gave him the key to my room and told him to go on ahead of me. I then headed to the hotel drugstore to buy a pack of condoms. The only ones they had were these god-awful aquamarine ribbed things. My God! I had never purchased a condom in my entire life, and here I was, a married woman, buying a pack of Trojans so I could have safe sex with some guy I had only met hours ago. I was totally out of my mind.

But I'll tell you Max, each and every second of that entire night is permanently etched in my memory. I keep remembering everything we did to each other. And I still don't know his name, and he doesn't know mine. He wanted to tell me his name, but I wouldn't let him. He wanted to continue the relationship—to see me again after that night—but I'm the one who said no.

I know this won't make any sense at all to you, but I *am* happily married. My husband is a wonderful man and we still enjoy being around each other after all these years. It's not as if we're bored with each other or that he treats me badly or anything like that. I think that's why I'm so torn up about the whole thing—I'm *not* unhappily married, so what I did makes no sense at all. I could never hurt my husband like that...or at least I thought I couldn't.

OTOH, I keep finding myself thinking about this

man, and wondering what he's doing, and where he is, and if he's thinking about me. Sometimes I wish I had taken his phone number just so I could pick up the phone and call him and hear his voice. It's driving me crazy, Max.

> Private Mail
> Date: Sunday, October 8, 1995 2:25 a.m.
> From: Maximilian@miller&morris.com
> Subj: Fear of Flying
> To: BevJ@frederic_gerard.com

Bev,

You must be going crazy, because I can see by your message headers that you're logging online from home on the weekends. You've always seemed so disciplined from the times on your messages—I mean, logging on from the office at 5 a.m. on weekdays? Cripes! Now you're sending me messages on a Saturday morning, so I know you must be upset.

I'm not sure what to tell you. Are you asking me what you should do, or are you just looking for a sympathetic ear? I'm sorry I gave you such a hard time in the beginning; I'm trying to get used to the idea. I'll promise to be as good a friend to you as I can, but I can't guarantee that I'll be much help.

Max

> Private Mail
> Date: Monday, October 9, 1995 8:34 a.m.
> From: BevJ@frederic_gerard.com
> Subj: Fear of Flying
> To: Maximilian@miller&morris.com

Thanks, Max. I think I'm just looking for someone to talk to. Obviously there's no way I can talk about it with Gary, and I can't tell any of my friends about it, either. I mean, they would totally freak out. I suppose the fact that you and I have never met F2F makes it a little easier for me to tell you these things.

Bev

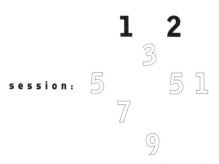

session:

1 2

> Private Mail
> Date: Monday, October 9, 1995 7:20 a.m.
> From: BevJ@frederic_gerard.com
> Subj: Goddamn Guy
> To: Maximilian@miller&morris.com

Max:

None of this really matters. I'll never see the guy
again anyway.

Maybe I could live with myself if I could just put the
whole thing out of my mind. You know, chalk it up
to the Stupid Mistakes category and forget about it.
Get on with my life. Go back to having fun and
enjoying life with Gary.

But I can't.

Saturday night Gary and I had rented a movie ("Farewell My Concubine"—it was pretty good). Anyhow, it was late, and we were huddled up next to each other on the couch eating Dove Bars watching the movie. We do this kind of thing a lot on weekends and it's usually really warm and intimate, but I have to tell you, my mind and my heart just weren't there. I was trying to pay attention to the movie, but when I was resting my head on Gary's shoulder, I kept thinking about the guy. The Goddamn Guy whose name I don't even know.

I wonder if he's thinking about me at all.

Bev

> Private Mail
> Date: Monday, October 9, 1995 10:29 a.m.
> From: Maximilian@miller&morris.com
> Subj: Goddamn Guy
> To: BevJ@frederic_gerard.com

Bev,

Do you think Gary suspects something is wrong?

Max

> Private Mail
> Date: Tuesday, October 10, 1995 8:12 a.m.
> From: BevJ@frederic_gerard.com
> Subj: Goddamn Guy
> To: Maximilian@miller&morris.com

I don't think so. I mean, there have been times in the past when I've had things on my mind and have just kind of faded for a while. But I always come back to life after a few days or weeks. I don't know how I'm going to yank myself out of this one, though. I'm in a major funk. I know it all must seem so stupid to you.

> Private Mail
> Date: Tuesday, October 10, 1995 11:36 a.m.
> From: Maximilian@miller&morris.com
> Subj: Goddamn Guy
> To: BevJ@frederic_gerard.com

No, Bev. It doesn't seem stupid to me. I just wish there was more I could do to help you through this.

Max

> Private Mail
> Date: Wednesday, October 11, 1995 8:12 a.m.
> From: BevJ@frederic_gerard.com
> Subj: Goddamn Guy
> To: Maximilian@miller&morris.com

Just be my friend and let me continue confiding in
you without judging me. There's no one else in the
world I could tell these things to. It sounds so
strange, but I really need you right now.

Bev

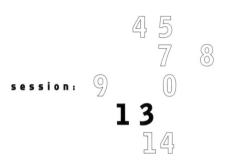

session: 13

> Private Mail
> Date: Wednesday, October 11, 1995 10:40 a.m.
> From: Maximilian@miller&morris.com
> Subj: Happy Birthday!
> To: BevJ@frederic_gerard.com

Hey Bev, isn't today your birthday? (It says your birthday is October 11th in your member profile.)

If so, HAPPY BIRTHDAY!!!

::: sending hugs across cyberspace :::

So what year were you born? <g,d&rvvf>

Max

> Private Mail
> Date: Wednesday, October 11, 1995 4:43 p.m.
> From: BevJ@frederic_gerard.com
> Subj: Happy Birthday!
> To: Maximilian@miller&morris.com

Yep, today's the day. <sigh> I just wish I was in a
better mood. Thanks for the birthday wishes anyway,
though.

::: returning hugs across cyberspace :::

I'm 36, in case you really wanted to know.

Bev

> Private Mail
> Date: Thursday, October 12, 1995 2:04 a.m.
> From: Maximilian@miller&morris.com
> Subj: Happy Birthday!
> To: BevJ@frederic_gerard.com

Boy, you must be *truly* upset—you're actually
answering my questions with straight answers. I
didn't expect you to answer that question about your
age—honest—I meant it as a joke. But, thanks for
answering anyway. That's about the age I thought
you were.

So, what can we talk about that will cheer you up?

How about if I let you ask me a question—any question?

p.s. I'm 32, if you were wondering.

> Private Mail
> Date: Thursday, October 12, 1995 6:53 a.m.
> From: BevJ@frederic_gerard.com
> Subj: 20 Questions
> To: Maximilian@miller&morris.com

OK, that sounds like fun. I'm trying to think of an interesting question...something that will make you squirm. <g>

p.s. I thought you'd be younger than that.

> Private Mail
> Date: Thursday, October 12, 1995 10:35 a.m.
> From: Maximilian@miller&morris.com
> Subj: 20 Questions
> To: BevJ@frederic_gerard.com

I guess I should take that as a compliment.

So what do you want to ask me?

::: squirming already :::

;-)

> Private Mail
> Date: Friday, October 13, 1995 7:55 a.m.
> From BevJ@frederic_gerard.com
> Subj: Boxers or Briefs?
> To: Maximilian@miller&morris.com

Max:

OK. I've come up with a question. Are you ready?

Do you wear boxer shorts or briefs?

> Private Mail
> Date: Friday, October 13, 1995 11:48 p.m.
> From: Maximilian@miller&morris.com
> Subj: Boxers or Briefs?
> To: BevJ@frederic_gerard.com

My, you're getting a little daring these days. When
we first started talking, you wouldn't even tell me
what your real name was. Now you want to know
what kind of underwear I wear?

> Private Mail
> Date: Saturday, October 14, 1995 11:00 a.m.
> From: BevJ@frederic_gerard.com
> Subj: Boxers or Briefs?
> To: Maximilian@miller&morris.com

Yeah. So, are you going to answer my question or not? I thought you said you wanted to cheer me up? <weg>

> Private Mail
> Date: Sunday, October 15, 1995 3:38 a.m.
> From: Maximilian@miller&morris.com
> Subj: Boxers or Briefs?
> To: BevJ@frederic_gerard.com

Bev,

You sure know how to take advantage of a situation—talk about striking while the iron is hot! ;-)

I wear boxers. In fact, I was wearing boxers long before it was cool to wear boxers. It all has to do with my Goldfish Theory.

> Private Mail
> Date: Monday, October 16, 1995 8:17 a.m.
> From: BevJ@frederic_gerard.com
> Subj: Boxers or Briefs?
> To: Maximilian@miller&morris.com

Hmmm. I pictured you as a briefs kind of guy. You know, like on the Calvin Klein ads. <g>

So what's this Goldfish Theory?

> Private Mail
> Date: Monday, October 16, 1995 10:49 a.m.
> From: Maximilian@miller&morris.com
> Subj: Max's Goldfish Theory
> To: BevJ@frederic_gerard.com

Oh yeah, well, did I tell you I used to be a model for Calvin Klein before I became a copywriter (and started wearing boxer shorts)? <vbg>

My Goldfish Theory. Well. Ahem. It relates very closely to every man's boxer-or-briefs dilemma. (Although if more men knew about my Goldfish Theory, no one would wear briefs anymore.)

It has to do with the premise that if you put a goldfish in a bowl that's too small, the goldfish will never get any bigger. So you have to keep your goldfish in a bowl that's much bigger than the fish. That way, your goldfish will have lots of room to grow.

Catch my drift?

Max

> Private Mail
> Date: Tuesday, October 17, 1995 8:13 a.m.
> From: BevJ@frederic_gerard.com
> Subj: Max's Goldfish Theory
> To: Maximilian@miller&morris.com

So, you seem to be concerned about the size of your fish. How does that make you feel?

<g,d&rvvf>

Bev

> Private Mail
> Date: Tuesday, October 17, 1995 10:24 a.m.
> From: Maximilian@miller&morris.com
> Subj: Max's Goldfish Theory
> To: BevJ@frederic_gerard.com

Well, well, well little missy. I hope you're having fun with yourself over there. <g>

Seriously, I'm glad I was able to cheer you up a bit.

Max

> Private Mail
> Date: Wednesday, October 18, 1995 8:34 a.m.
> From: BevJ@frederic_gerard.com
> Subj: Thanks
> To: Maximilian@miller&morris.com

You have, Max. Thanks.

Bev

> Private Mail
> Date: Wednesday, October 18, 1995 10:28 a.m.
> From: Maximilian@miller&morris.com
> Subj: Thanks
> To: BevJ@frederic_gerard.com

So does that mean you'll tell me what kind of underwear you wear?

> Private Mail
> Date: Thursday, October 19, 1995 7:30 a.m.
> From: BevJ@frederic_gerard.com
> Subj: Thanks
> To: Maximilian@miller&morris.com

Not very likely.

> Private Mail
> Date: Thursday, October 19, 1995 10:59 a.m.
> From: Maximilian@miller&morris.com
> Subj: Thanks
> To: BevJ@frederic_gerard.com

Well at least you didn't give me an absolute, flat-out
no...

}:-)

12
14
3 15
1 7
8

> Private Mail
> Date: Friday, October 20, 1995 11:56 p.m.
> From: Maximilian@miller&morris.com
> Subj: Hiya
> To: BevJ@frederic_gerard.com

Hi Bev,

So how are you doing?

Max

> Private Mail
> Date: Saturday, October 21, 1995 10:02 a.m.
> From: BevJ@frederic_gerard.com
> Subj: Hiya
> To: Maximilian@miller&morris.com

Ohhh...OK I guess. What are you up to?

> Private Mail
> Date: Saturday, October 21, 1995 10:46 a.m.
> From: Maximilian@miller&morris.com
> Subj: Hiya
> To: BevJ@frederic_gerard.com

Not too much. Trying to figure out some HTML
stuff. Drinking coffee, bumming around. My usual
Saturday morning antics.

Are you logging on from home or from the office?

> Private Mail
> Date: Saturday, October 21, 1995 11:08 a.m.
> From: BevJ@frederic_gerard.com
> Subj: Hiya
> To: Maximilian@miller&morris.com

I'm logging on from home. Gary's away on a business
trip, so I'm hanging out in my home office, aimlessly
wading through the information ocean. :-)

So, what—are you going to create your own Web page or something?

> Private Mail
> Date: Saturday, October 21, 1995 11:21 a.m.
> From: Maximilian@miller&morris.com
> Subj: Hiya
> To: BevJ@frederic_gerard.com

Yeah, actually I am (thinking of creating my own Web page).

We seem to be online at the same time. Why don't you give me your phone number—let me call you right now, so we can chat "live," and hear each other's voices?

> Private Mail
> Date: Saturday, October 21, 1995 12:13 p.m.
> From BevJ@frederic_gerard.com
> Subj: Hiya
> To: Maximilian@miller&morris.com

No.

> Private Mail
> Date: Saturday, October 21, 1995 1:06 p.m.
> From: Maximilian@miller&morris.com
> Subj: Hiya
> To: BevJ@frederic_gerard.com

Ooooooookay. Guess you're pretty much opposed to
that idea. <g>

So tell me something.

> Private Mail
> Date: Saturday, October 21, 1995 3:17 p.m.
> From: BevJ@frederic_gerard.com
> Subj: Hiya
> To: Maximilian@miller&morris.com

Now what do you want to know? <g>

(Really, I've told you all of my secrets. There's nothing interesting left to tell.)

> Private Mail
> Date: Saturda, October 21, 1995 3:38 a.m.
> From: Maximilian@miller&morris.com
> Subj: Hiya
> To: BevJ@frederic_gerard.com

No, it's nothing that personal. I just want to know

what you get from being online. I've been thinking about it myself lately, and I'm curious as to what other people gain from this whole online thing.

> Private Mail
> Date: Saturday, October 21, 1995 4:21 p.m.
> From: BevJ@frederic_gerard.com
> Subj: Junkie?
> To: Maximilian@miller&morris.com

That's a fairly easy question, compared to the ones you've been asking me. <g> So I'll give it a shot.

I originally got "online" because I had to. Several years ago I had a boss who was really into Compu-Serve, so we all got accounts and had to learn our way around. At first I found dealing with modems and telecommunications protocols extremely mysteri-ous and frustrating. But once I overcame the initial problems, I guess you could say I sort of fell into the groove. I got my current book publisher turned on to CompuServe and we've been on the Net for a couple of years now.

I get a real charge out of "talking" to people from all over the world, so I've been logging on almost every weekday ever since I started. I like reading about what people on the other side of the world are doing and thinking, and I feel as if logging on to the Net or CIS helps me keep my finger on the pulse of the world. I even log onto AOL occasionally.

I'm sure there's more to it than that, though. I sometimes think I've become a communications junkie.
No—let me take that back. I've *always* been a communications junkie. Except before, I would write a
lot of letters and talk on the phone all the time. Now
all I have to do is log on to some forum or news-
group and I'm instantly in the middle of a communications orgy. <g>

How about you—why did you get online?

> Private Mail
> Date: Saturday, October 21, 1995 5:33 p.m.
> From: Maximilian@miller&morris.com
> Subj: Junkie?
> To: BevJ@frederic_gerard.com

I must admit my getting online had very little to do
with work or professional improvement. Mostly I
think it was something like penis envy—several of
my friends would be talking about their 14.4 and
28.8 baud modems and I guess I felt a little left out.
I mean, we used to hang out in bars together and
talk about chicks and cars and sports, and now
everybody's talking about modem speeds, RAM, and
hard drives.

Remember the 1970s Corvettes, with the really long
front ends? We used to call them Penis Extenders.
Nowadays all the guys I know drive minivans. But
being men, we still need our Penis Extenders. So we

go out and buy these shit-hot computers with CD-ROM drives, 32-bit color, and more memory than we could ever even dream of using.

Me, I am now the proud owner of a *screamingly* fast modem. But I've still got my old '386. <g>

> Private Mail
> Date: Saturday, October 21, 1995 6:50 p.m.
> From: BevJ@frederic_gerard.com
> Subj: Junkie?
> To: Maximilian@miller&morris.com

Then I guess you're not so worried about the size of your goldfish after all. ;-)

> Private Mail
> Date: Saturday, October 21, 1995 8:41 p.m.
> From: Maximilian@miller&morris.com
> Subj: Junkie?
> To: BevJ@frederic_gerard.com

You're absolutely right! ;-)

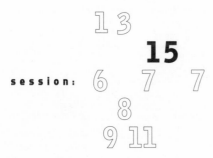

session: **15**

> Private Mail
> Date: Wednesday, October 25, 1995 8:57 a.m.
> From: BevJ@frederic_gerard.com
> Subj: Just Checking In
> To: Maximilian@miller&morris.com

Max:

Haven't heard from you in a few days and wondering
if you're all right.

Everything here is OK. Work's going well. Gary's
fine. I'm still pretty much in a complete twist over
the Goddamn Guy, but am trying to get over it
(though not having much luck).

Hope everything's fine with you.

Bev

> Private Mail
> Date: Thursday, October 26, 1995 11:07 a.m.
> From: Maximilian@miller&morris.com
> Subj: Just Checking In
> To: BevJ@frederic_gerard.com

So you've still got that Goddamn Guy on your mind, huh? He must have been one hell of a dude.

Everything here sucks. I think I'm going to get fired. As I told you, things weren't going exactly swimmingly at work to begin with. Then I kinda went on this minor binge and missed the last three days of work.

When I came in this morning, people were avoiding me in the hallways and whispering stuff. I'm pretty sure my ass is grass.

Max

> Private Mail
> Date: Friday, October 27, 1995 6:16 a.m.
> From: BevJ@frederic_gerard.com
> Subj: Just Checking In
> To: Maximilian@miller&morris.com

What do you mean, you "kinda went on this minor
binge and missed the last three days of work"? You
call that a minor binge?

Max, what's wrong? Something else must be bothering you.

Bev

> Private Mail
> Date: Friday, October 27, 1995 10:18 a.m.
> From: Maximilian@miller&morris.com
> Subj: Just Checking In
> To: BevJ@frederic_gerard.com

I *have* been pretty bummed out lately, Bev, but I
didn't want to dump it on you since you were having
your own troubles.

Max

> Private Mail
> Date: Friday, October 27, 1995 4:36 p.m.
> From BevJ@frederic_gerard.com
> Subj: Just Checking In
> To: Maximilian@miller&morris.com

Maybe it would help me to forget about my own
problems for a while and try to help someone else.
What's up?

I take it you haven't been fired yet, seeing as you're
still logging on from work.

Bev

> Private Mail
> Date: Saturday, October 28, 1995 1:06 a.m.
> From: Maximilian@miller&morris.com
> Subj: Luv Sucks
> To: BevJ@frederic_gerard.com

No, I haven't been shit-canned yet. I did get called
into my boss' office yesterday, and he screamed at me
for about an hour. It was real weird. It's like it could
have been anybody sitting there; the guy just gets off
on trying to humiliate people. So I just sat there and
closed in on myself and waited 'til he was done rant-
ing and raving.

But that's not really why I'm upset.

> Private Mail
> Date: Saturday, October 28, 1995 9:44 a.m.
> From: BevJ@frederic_gerard.com
> Subj: Luv Sucks
> To: Maximilian@miller&morris.com

Well, Max, it's not as if your boss didn't have a reason to be pissed at you. I mean, you didn't show up
at work for three days, right?

But what's this *really* about? From the way you
changed the message header, I gather you're having
some sort of romantic difficulties.

> Private Mail
> Date: Saturday, October 28, 1995 1:27 p.m.
> From: Maximilian@miller&morris.com
> Subj: Luv Sucks
> To: BevJ@frederic_gerard.com

Right, and right.

> Private Mail
> Date: Saturday, October 28, 1995 4:49 p.m.
> From: BevJ@frederic_gerard.com
> Subj: Luv Sucks
> To: Maximilian@miller&morris.com

So what the hell is going on? Are you going to make

me keep guessing, or will I have to pry this out of you?

And how can you say "Luv Sucks" if you've told me you've never been in love before?

Bev

> Private Mail
> Date: Saturday, October 28, 1995 6:01 p.m.
> From: Maximilian@miller&morris.com
> Subj: Luv Sucks
> To: BevJ@frederic_gerard.com

Because I've changed my mind.

Look, Bev. I'm having second thoughts. Maybe we shouldn't talk about this right now.

Max

> Private Mail
> Date: Saturday, October 28, 1995 6:54 p.m.
> From: BevJ@frederic_gerard.com
> Subj: Luv Sucks?
> To: Maximilian@miller&morris.com

What do you mean, you've changed your mind?

You've changed your mind about whether or not love sucks, or whether or not you've ever been in love?

You can't back out now, buster. We're going to talk about this.

I've got an idea—why don't we have a live chat?

> Private Mail
> Date: Saturday, October 28, 1995 7:23 p.m.
> From: Maximilian@miller&morris.com
> Subj: Luv Sucks?
> To: BevJ@frederic_gerard.com

You mean you'll let me call you?

> Private Mail
> Date: Saturday, October 28, 1995 7:42 p.m.
> From: BevJ@frederic_gerard.com
> Subj: Luv Sucks?
> To: Maximilian@miller&morris.com

No. I mean we can chat online "live." As opposed to sending e-mails back and forth, when you're having a real-time chat, you can instantly see what the other person has typed into the little dialog box as soon as they hit the return key. Why don't you meet me in the Writer's Forum at 9:00 p.m. EST? When I see

that you've logged on, I'll initiate a "chat session"—
no one else will be able to see our conversation
except you and me.

OK?

> Private Mail
> Date: Saturday, October 28, 1995 8:05 p.m.
> From: Maximilian@miller&morris.com
> Subj: Luv Sucks?
> To: BevJ@frederic_gerard.com

Bev,

OK. See you there.

Max

14
5 **1** **6** 3
5
7 8

> Saturday, October 28, 1995 9:02 p.m.

> Writer's Forum   > Live Chat   > People Here: 2

(Private)

BevJ:	So you made it.
Maximilan:	Yeah—this is pretty wild. How come we never did this before?
BevJ:	Dunno.
Maximilan:	It's kind of like the live conferences, except this is totally private, right?
BevJ:	Right.
Maximilan:	What do I do if I have to go the bathroom or go get a martini?

BevJ:	You just type AFK, which means Away From Keyboard. The other person will then know that you're not at your computer and it may be a while before you respond. I use it a lot when I'm online and my phone rings—I just type AFK and the other person knows I won't be typing for a few minutes.
Maximilian:	This is addicting. I can see my bills for online time getting bigger by the minute.
BevJ:	Yeah, that's one of the drawbacks of talking "live"—the clock keeps ticking while you're typing. It's much less expensive to compose messages offline and then send them all in one session.
Maximilian:	Although talking "live" like this would seem to be a much better way to have cybersex. ;-)
BevJ:	I wouldn't know.
Maximilian:	So you're telling me you've been online all these years and have never done the cybersex thing?
BevJ:	Nope. Until my recent incident, I've always been faithful.
Maximilian:	So let's talk more about that.
BevJ:	Max, we didn't come here to talk about me—we're supposed to be talking about you and your situation. What's going on?
Maximilian:	Wellll...remember when I told you I had never been in love before?
BevJ:	Yes.

Maximilian:	I think I've fallen in love with someone since then.
BevJ:	You're kidding! How come you didn't tell me you had met someone?
Maximilian:	Lots of reasons, I guess. I always worried that I wouldn't recognize being in love when it happened, but it has finally happened and I'm completely in love. I mean, this is it. She's the one. I love this woman.
BevJ:	What's she like?
Maximilian:	She's beautiful. And I don't mean just her looks. She's smart, she's funny, she's compassionate, she's together, and she's absolutely *wicked* in bed. }:-) I worship her.
BevJ:	So what's the problem?
Maximilian:	She won't let me call her.
BevJ:	Well that's weird. Isn't she in love with you?
Maximilian:	I think she is. She hasn't admitted it, but I do think she's in love with me.
BevJ:	Are you sure this woman isn't just blowing you off, Max?
Maxmilian:	I'm sure.
BevJ:	Then why won't she let you call her?
Maximilian:	Part of it is that I don't have her phone number.
BevJ:	You've been sleeping with a woman and yet you don't have her phone number? I don't get it.
Maximilian:	We were only together one night. I met her at Macworld. At the Fractal Party.

	The Boston Computer Museum. She wouldn't even tell me her name, or let me tell her mine. But it was the most wonderful night of my life. I love her.
Maximilian:	Bev, are you there?
BevJ:	You son of a bitch.
Maximilian:	Bev, I know it was you. I'm in love with you. Can't we just meet somewhere and talk about this? Won't you at least let me call you? I love you and I want to be with you. This is making me crazy. I can't sleep. I can't do anything at work. All I want to do is sit at my computer and wait for your next message.
BevJ:	Max, stop.
Maximilian:	I dream about the night we spent together. It was perfect. Your body is perfect. Your mind is perfect. I want to know everything about you. I can still remember the smell of your perfume. I even stole the pillowcase from the hotel room where you rested your head, so I can smell you every night when I try to go to sleep. But all I do is lie awake and think about you.
BevJ:	So that's where the pillowcase went... I can't believe this is happening.
Maximilian:	Bev, I—
BevJ:	Stop it, Max! I don't want to hear it! You goddamned son of a bitch. How long have you known it was me? And you let me make a fool of myself, let

	me talk about my innermost feelings without knowing it was you? You fucking asshole!
Maximilian:	Bev, I swear, I didn't know it was you right away. I only realized it was you when you began telling me the details of the affair. I didn't even *ask* you for details—you volunteered them! But once I read your message describing the night we spent together, there was no turning back. I didn't know what to do. I didn't want our online friendship to end because then I would lose you completely. So I decided to simply not say anything. But then it got to the point where I couldn't stand it any longer. I swear I wasn't trying to make a fool of you, Bev. I love you.
BevJ:	I don't want to talk about this anymore. I have to go, Max.
Maximilian:	No Bev! Please—don't go.
%System%:	BevJ has left the forum.

online glossary

acronyms & abbreviations

AFK	away from keyboard
AOL	America Online
BG	big grin
BPS	bits per second
BTW	by the way
CIS	CompuServe Information Service
CUL	see you later
CULA	see you later alligator
F2F	face-to-face
FWIW	for what it's worth
FYI	for your information
G	grin
G,D&R	grinning, ducking & running
G,D&RVVF	grinning, ducking & running very very fast
GA	go ahead
GMTA	great minds think alike

HTML	HyperText Markup Language
IMA	I might add
IMHO	in my humble opinion
IMNSHO	in my not-so-humble opinion
IMO	in my opinion
LOL	laughing out loud
Net	short for Internet
OTOH	on the other hand
PMFJI	pardon me for jumping in
ROFLOL	rolling on floor laughing out loud
RSN	real soon now
TIA	thanks in advance
TPTB	the powers that be
VBG	very big grin
Web	short for World Wide Web
WEG	wicked evil grin
WWW	World Wide Web

emoticons & other symbols

:-)	smile
;-)	wink
:-(	frown
:-*	kiss
:'-(	crying
}:-)	horny smile
< > or :: ::	signifies something that the writer is pretending to do or say, such as <sigh> or ::going to get body oil now::
>>>>	indicates the words following this symbol are being quoted from another message
* * or _ _	indicate that the word or phrase typed inside these symbols should be emphasized

colophon

This book was written, produced, and packaged by Rainwater Press in Denver, Colorado using a Macintosh Quadra 650 with 32MB RAM and a 230MB hard drive, a SyQuest 5200C external drive, and a Global Village Platinum 28.8 fax/modem. Text was composed using Microsoft Word version 5.1 and page layouts were created using QuarkXPress version 3.31. Preliminary page proofs were printed from a 600-dpi HP LaserJet4 laser printer.

The cover and interior page templates were designed by High Design in Ocala, Florida using Adobe Illustrator and QuarkXPress for Macintosh. The typeface used in the title on the front cover is a shareware typeface called Faktos; the chapter heads were designed using Faktos and Bell Gothic Black; the body text is set in Adobe Caslon and Adobe Caslon Expert.

Rainwater Press
P.O. Box 200695
Denver, CO 80220 USA
(800) 269-9715 (phone)
(303) 377-9424 (fax)
http://www.rainwater.com

High Design
405 Southeast 49th Ave.
Ocala, FL 34471 USA
(352) 624-0088 (phone)
(352) 624-0086 (fax)

ABOUT THE AUTHOR

NAN MCCARTHY WAS BORN IN CHICAGO IN 1961.
SHE OWNS RAINWATER PRESS, AN INDEPENDENT
PUBLISHING FIRM SHE FOUNDED IN 1992.
NAN IS THE AUTHOR AND ART DIRECTOR OF
QUARK DESIGN, A FOUR-COLOR GUIDE TO PAGE
LAYOUT SOFTWARE FOR DESIGNERS PUBLISHED BY
PEACHPIT PRESS IN THE U.S. AND BY
GRAPHIC-SHA PUBLISHING IN JAPAN. SHE IS A
COLUMNIST FOR DYNAMIC GRAPHICS MAGAZINE
AND CONTRIBUTES TO SEVERAL OTHER DESIGN-
AND PUBLISHING-RELATED MAGAZINES.
THIS IS HER FIRST WORK OF FICTION.
HER WEB SITE IS LOCATED AT:
HTTP://WWW.RAINWATER.COM